# Indianapolis

# Indianapolis

## A Downtown America Book

S.L. Berry

**ⅆP** Dillon Press, Inc.   Minneapolis, MN   55415

For her humor, love, and support, this book is
dedicated to Margo.

## Photographic Acknowledgments

Photos have been reproduced through the courtesy
of Darryl Jones, Patty Lindley, Bass Photo Collec-
tion (neg. #66756F)/Indiana Historical Society (neg.
#C2140), Chris Minnick, The Indianapolis Zoo,
The Indianapolis Children's Choir, and Indiana
Black Expo. Cover photo by Darryl Jones.

**Library of Congress Cataloging-in-Publication Data**

Berry, S. L.
    Indianapolis / S.L. Berry.
      p.   cm. — (A Downtown America book)
    Summary: Explores the city of Indianapolis, both past and
present, describing neighborhoods, attractions, festivals, and
historic sites.
    ISBN 0-87518-426-X (lib. bdg.) : $12.95
    1. Indianapolis (Ind.)—Juvenile literature. [1. Indianapolis
(Ind.)]   I. Title.   II. Series.
F534.I34B47   1990
977.2—dc20                                          89-25693
                                                        CIP
                                                        AC

Dillon Press, Inc., 242 Portland Avenue South
Minneapolis, Minnesota  55415

Printed in the United States of America
1  2  3  4  5  6  7  8  9  10  99  98  97  96  95  94  93  92  91  90

## About the Author

Skip Berry is an editorial consultant
for a variety of advertising agencies,
public relations firms, and businesses
in the Indianapolis area. His writing
credits include numerous articles in
publications such as *The New York
Times*, *The Chicago Tribune*, and *Indianapolis Magazine*.

Mr. Berry is a former writer-in-resi-
dence for a variety of elementary and
middle schools in Indianapolis, and is
a long-time resident of the city.

# Contents

City Flag.

City Seal.

# Fast Facts about Indianapolis

**Indianapolis:** Indy; Circle City; Amateur Sports Capital of the World; Crossroads of America

**Location:** Central Indiana, on the west fork of the White River

**Area:** City, 405 square miles (1,049 square kilometers); metropolitan area, 3,089 square miles (8,000 square kilometers)

**Population (1986 estimate\*):** City, 720,000; metropolitan area, 1,228,600

**Major Population Groups:** Whites, Blacks, Hispanics, Asians

**Altitude:** Highest point, 840 feet (256 meters) above sea level; lowest point, 700 feet (214 meters) above sea level

**Climate:** Average temperature in January is 26°F (-3°C), 75°F (24°C) in July; average annual precipitation is 40 inches (1 meter)

**Founding Date:** 1822; chartered as a city in 1847

**City Flag:** A small, white five-pointed star sits in a red circle on a field of blue; one white vertical stripe and one white horizontal stripe meet at the red circle, surrounding it; the star symbolizes Indianapolis's position as state capital; the white stripes represent the city's crossroads reputation

**City Seal:** A gold circle in the middle of which is an eagle carrying the scales of justice in its talons; "City of Indianapolis" is printed around the top of the circle, and "Indiana" is at the bottom

**Form of Government:** Indianapolis and surrounding Marion County are combined to form *Unigov*; a mayor and 29 council members are elected to four-year terms

**Important Industries:** Manufacturing, transportation, medicine, sports

\*U.S. Bureau of the Census 1990 census figures available in 1991-92.

## Festivals and Parades

**March:** St. Patrick's Day parade

**May:** Broad Ripple Art Fair; Indianapolis 500 Festival and parade

**June:** Midsummer Festival; Italian Street Festival

**July:** Indiana Black Expo's Summer Celebration

**August:** Indiana State Fair at the state fairgrounds; Circle Fest

**September:** Penrod Days Art Fair; Greek Festival; Fiesta Indianapolis

**October:** International Festival

**November:** Veteran's Day parade

**December:** World's Largest Christmas Tree at Soldiers and Sailors Monument

For further information about festivals and parades, see agencies listed on page 56.

# United States

# Indianapolis

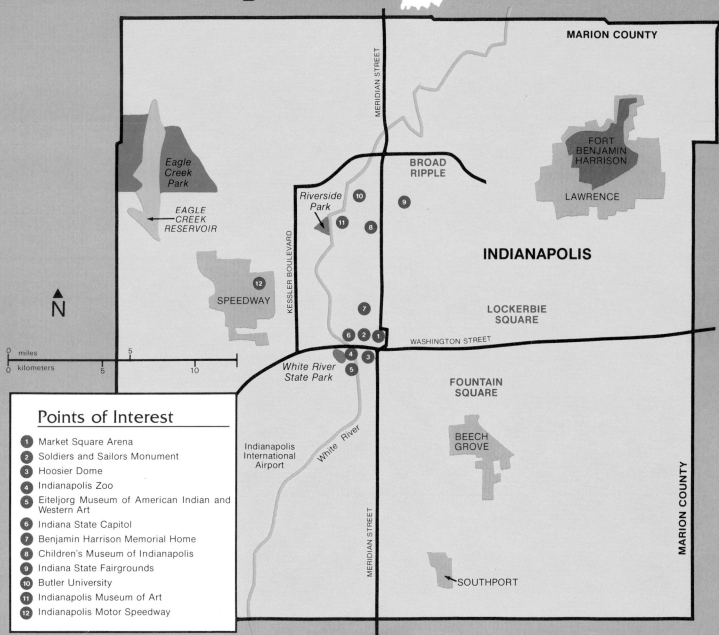

INDIANA
● Indianapolis

MARION COUNTY

Eagle Creek Park

EAGLE CREEK RESERVOIR

⑩

Riverside Park

⑪

⑫

SPEEDWAY

⑧

BROAD RIPPLE

⑨

FORT BENJAMIN HARRISON

LAWRENCE

INDIANAPOLIS

LOCKERBIE SQUARE

⑦

KESSLER BOULEVARD

N

miles
0 ——————— 5
kilometers
0 ——————— 5 ——————— 10

⑥ ② ①

④ ③

⑤

WASHINGTON STREET

White River State Park

Indianapolis International Airport

White River

MERIDIAN STREET

FOUNTAIN SQUARE

BEECH GROVE

SOUTHPORT

MARION COUNTY

## Points of Interest

1. Market Square Arena
2. Soldiers and Sailors Monument
3. Hoosier Dome
4. Indianapolis Zoo
5. Eiteljorg Museum of American Indian and Western Art
6. Indiana State Capitol
7. Benjamin Harrison Memorial Home
8. Children's Museum of Indianapolis
9. Indiana State Fairgrounds
10. Butler University
11. Indianapolis Museum of Art
12. Indianapolis Motor Speedway

Young people play in University Park. The Indianapolis War Memorial stands in the background.

walnuts shade lawns and homes. In the spring, pink and white dogwood trees flower all over town.

Grassy park areas and gardens bright with flowers attract downtown office workers to University Park. In the summertime, this park is full of lunchtime picnickers listening to live jazz. In the autumn, entire city blocks glow with the golden-orange light of the fall leaves. In wintertime, tiny white lights twinkle on trees all over the Mile Square.

Indianapolis's winter tempera-

as the Amateur Sports Capital of the World due to the many sporting events that take place here. It is known as the Circle City, too, because of the way the city was first designed.

A surveyor named Alexander Ralston planned Indianapolis. He designed it as a square with sides one mile (1.6 kilometers) long. In the center of that square, now called the Mile Square, Ralston designed a wide street circling a wooded hill. Other streets ran out from this circle like the spokes on a wheel. Today, this is known as Monument Circle. It is the home of one of the city's best-known landmarks, the Soldiers and Sailors Monument. The monument honors those who fought in the Mexican,

Civil, and Spanish-American wars.

Until skyscrapers came along, the Monument was the tallest building in Indiana. The look-out tower on the top floor of the 284-foot (86.6-kilometer) memorial still gives visitors a nice view of downtown Indianapolis.

While the view from the monument is good, the view from the twenty-eighth floor of the City-County Building is even better. The land rolls gently in a few places, but most of Indianapolis is built on flat ground. From 28 stories up, the city spreads out like a giant jigsaw puzzle.

What it lacks in hills, Indianapolis makes up for in greenery. Once, the city was a thick forest. Today, it is still filled with trees. In older neighborhoods, large oaks, maples, and

The Soldiers and Sailors Monument is a landmark in Indianpolis.

# 1

# More Than a Speedway

When you hear the name *Indianapolis*, what do you think of? Do you imagine brightly-colored race cars roaring around an oval track at great speeds? If you do, you are not alone. Most Americans know Indianapolis only as the home of the Indianapolis 500. Each year, thousands come to the city to watch one of the best-known auto races in the world. But Indianapolis has much more to offer.

The capital of Indiana, Indianapolis is the thirteenth largest city in the country. It is also home to more than 720,000 people. Most can trace their roots back to such countries as Italy, Germany, France, Ireland, and Hungary. Blacks make up more than 21 percent of the population. The city is also home to smaller Hispanic and Asian ethnic groups.

Indianapolis has become known

Skyscrapers rise from the changing skyline of downtown Indianapolis.

A hot dog vendor winds his way through Mile Square.

tures usually fall below 20°F (7°C) for only a few days at a time. In the summertime, it rarely gets hotter than 90°F (32°C) for very long. The city gets an average of 40 inches (1 meter) of rain a year. That's enough to keep the greenery green, the flowers in bloom, and the city's residents and visitors happy.

More people than ever are visiting Indianapolis these days. One reason for this is the wide variety of things to do in the city. One of the most popular attractions—besides

Crowds gather at the Indianapolis Museum of Art.

the Indy 500—is the Children's Museum of Indianapolis. This museum is the largest of its kind in the world. People also come here to see the Eiteljorg Museum of American Indian and Western Art, and the Indianapolis Museum of Art. At Connor Prairie, visitors can see what life was like in the 1800s.

In downtown Indianapolis, Union Station attracts people to its many restaurants and shops. Once, though, it was a very busy railroad station. Union Station is one example of the

many buildings that have been restored in Indianapolis in past years. This has made the city more attractive to residents and new industries.

Since the late 1960s, many new businesses have moved to Indianapolis. These include publishing and videotape production companies, computer software designers, robotics firms, electronics companies, and many different manufacturers. A large number of sporting organizations have also come to the city.

In the 170 years since Jonathan Jennings, Indiana's first governor, helped to create a capital city in the center of Indiana, Indianapolis has developed from a small clump of cabins into one of the fastest growing cities in the Midwest. Today's Indianapolis gives its citizens and its tourists more to look forward to than Governor Jennings ever dreamed of.

# 2

# Creating a City

In 1820, Governor Jonathan Jennings wanted to move Indiana's capital from the small village of Corydon to the center of the state. That way, it would be the same traveling distance for residents who lived near the state's borders. Jennings sent 10 commissioners to find a site for the new capital. They chose an area where Fall Creek and the White River meet in the center of Indiana.

The commissioners thought that people and supplies could be moved in and out of the area by river. They found out later that they were wrong. The White River was, and still is, too shallow for anything but small boats.

After the site for the city had been chosen, it was up to the Indiana General Assembly to choose its name. After days of arguing over possible names, Judge Jeremiah Sullivan came

Boys dressed in 19th century-style clothing play on the grounds at Connor Prairie.

up with the name that was finally used. He joined that state's name—*Indiana*—with the Greek name for city—*polis*—and Indianapolis was born, at least in spirit.

Even with a name, Indianapolis was still more of an idea than a city. State officials hired Alexander Ralston to draw up a plan for the capital. Ralston had worked with Charles L'Enfant, a surveyor who had designed Washington, D.C. When Ralston was finished drawing up his plan for the city, it looked a lot like the layout for the nation's capital.

The challenge of creating a city out of the forest drew people to the Indianapolis area. Early settlers turned trees into cabins, trails into streets, and Ralston's plan into a town.

By 1824, almost 700 people called Indianapolis home.

The completion of two roads in the 1830s, the National Highway and the Michigan Road, helped make Indianapolis a transportation center. Over the next few years, more roads were cut through the wilderness. Many started in, ended at, or passed through Indianapolis.

Work on a rail line between Indianapolis and the southern Indiana town of Madison began in 1839. The construction of this railroad, as well as other building projects, brought hundreds of immigrants to Indianapolis. Two groups, the Irish and the Germans, had a great effect on the young city. Their hard work helped the city grow and develop.

When Indianapolis became a city in 1847, residents elected their first mayor. At the same time, the people voted to create a public school system. It was one of the first in the country.

During the Civil War, Indianapolis was an important center for the Union Army. Trainloads of Union soldiers on their way to battle or on their way home stopped in the city. Camp Morton, which had been used as a training camp before the war, was turned into a prison for Confederate soldiers.

At this time, Indianapolis residents also took part in the national debate about slavery. In the city, pro-slavery forces and abolitionists (people against slavery) such as Ovid But-

ler argued over human rights. Hiram Bacon's dairy farm, just east of the city, served as a way-station for the Underground Railroad. This was the name for the system used to smuggle escaped slaves to freedom in the North.

After the Civil War, Indianapolis streets were crowded with ex-soldiers, freed slaves, European immigrants, and newcomers from the East Coast. People came to Indianapolis to take advantage of the many business opportunities in the city.

Between 1870 and 1900, immigrants continued to make their way to Indianapolis. Among these were Italian tailors, shoemakers, barbers, fruit and vegetable dealers, and musicians. Greek merchants and mechanics

Madame C.J. Walker.

came, too. By 1910, Armenians, Hungarians, Poles, and other eastern Europeans had arrived in the city. They took jobs in the factories at first. When they could, they set up small shops of their own.

In addition to the European immigrants, blacks were also helping to shape the city. Madame C.J. Walker's hair care products for blacks were making her well known in Indianapolis and other parts of the country. The company was one of the most famous black-owned businesses at the turn of the century. Madame Walker was the country's first black female millionaire.

As many other blacks began to open businesses northeast of Mile Square, neighborhoods grew. Indiana

Avenue became the main street in a busy, lively community. The rise of jazz in the 1920s brought national attention to the area. Some of the best-known jazz musicians of the time came to Indianapolis to play in the clubs on Indiana Avenue.

The Indianapolis Motor Speedway was built in 1909. Two years later, the first 500-mile (805-kilometer) auto race was held there. Ray Harroun won that first race, driving a black and yellow Marmon Wasp to victory at an average speed of 74.9 miles (120.6 kilometers) per hour. Today, Indy cars race at speeds of more than 200 miles (322 kilometers) per hour.

When the United States entered World War I in 1917, Indianapolis played an important role. Local factories made ammunition and engines for aircraft and land vehicles. The city was also a connecting point for trains carrying troops and freight.

During World War II, the city became "Toolmaker to the Nation." Every Indianapolis resident who was old enough to work found a job. Factories ran 24 hours a day. Each day, workers made transportation equipment, weapons parts, and aircraft engines.

The end of World War II was also the end of Indianapolis's importance as a railway center. As people turned to cars and airplanes for cross-country travel, the railroads lost passengers. When many of the railroad companies went out of business, Indi-

anapolis lost the hustle and bustle of trains coming and going.

By the 1960s, the Indianapolis 500 had become the city's main claim to fame. People thought of Indianapolis as a city that woke up every May for the auto race, then went back to sleep for the rest of the year. People began calling it "Naptown."

But Indianapolis isn't napping any longer. In 1970, the governments of Indianapolis and surrounding Marion County combined to form "Unigov." Unigov stands for "unified government." Under this system, the mayor of Indianapolis and a city-county council make decisions about such things as taxes, building projects, housing developments, and social programs. Because of this, city officials and business leaders have been able to carry out many projects that have changed both the look and the spirit of Indianapolis.

By combining city and county tax funds, Unigov gave Indianapolis more money. This money helped new businesses to move to the city. It also helped pay for building the Hoosier Dome and several new Olympic-quality sports centers. Since 1970, many national and international sporting events have been held in the city. As more people have begun visiting the city for these events, new hotels and restaurants have opened.

Millions of dollars have been spent repairing old buildings and constructing new ones. The city's skyline has changed quickly as new office

One of the first runnings of the Indianapolis 500.

towers have been built all over the Mile Square.

Today, Indianapolis has a new look. Yet there is still work to do. As with any large city, Indianapolis has problems that can't be solved by putting up a new building. The need for low-income housing, the growing teenage pregnancy rate, and the quality of education in public schools are just some of the residents' concerns.

With the growth of new businesses in the city, though, there is more money to help solve the city's problems. New community programs, too, are helping to keep Indianapolis on the move. Together, Indianapolis citizens and city officials are looking toward a bright future.

The Hoosier Dome is one of many new buildings erected in Indianapolis in the 1980s.

# 3

# A National Crossroads

In the late 1800s, Indianapolis stood in the center of a web of train tracks. Since then, the city has been a transportation center. A century ago, dozens of railroad routes passed through Indianapolis. This gave the city the nickname, "Crossroads of America."

Today, most of the rail lines are gone. Yet more than a dozen highways now cross in Indianapolis. These roads have made trucking a big indus-

try in the city. Mayflower Corporation, one of the largest trucking firms in the United States, is based here.

Though not as important as they once were, trains still help meet people's needs. Five rail lines carry passengers and freight in and out of the city.

In the late nineteenth century, Indianapolis was also a transport center of another sort. A large number of carriage and bicycle makers had

Once a busy train depot, Union Station is now filled with shops, restaurants, and even a hotel.

factories in the city. This helped Indianapolis become an early leader in the auto industry.

In 1899, carriage maker Charles Black built the first Indianapolis "horseless carriage," as cars were called. After Black, other inventors and mechanics became involved in automaking. Before long, the city was one of the leading carmakers in the country. Between 1900 and 1936, 64 automaking companies were based in Indianapolis. However, after Henry Ford improved the assembly line, most of these moved to Detroit.

One company that is still involved in carmaking in Indianapolis is General Motors Corporation. In their Speedway plants, employees still design and make vehicle parts.

Today, Indianapolis's economy relies more on air transportation than trains or cars. The country's largest charter airline, American Trans Air, is based at the Indianapolis International Airport. Also, the nation's first modern helicopter landing field, the Indianapolis Downtown Heliport, is near the Mile Square.

Medicine has also been important to Indianapolis's growth. One of the world's largest prescription drug companies, Eli Lilly & Company, has had its headquarters in Indianapolis since 1876. That year, the company's founder, Eli Lilly, opened his shop on a downtown street. Lilly had three employees then. Today, Eli Lilly & Company employs more than 7,000 people. Its offices, research laboratories, and production plants spread out over several square blocks.

Other medical businesses in Indianapolis include medical equipment maker Boehringer Manheim. Also, the Indiana University Medical Center is one of the most respected medical research and training centers in the United States.

Perhaps because of these medical centers, health and physical fitness are important to many Indianapolis residents. From early in the morning until late at night, people fill the city's many fitness clubs. There are also several indoor and outdoor tennis and basketball courts, as well as swimming pools.

This interest in sports can be seen all around Indianapolis. The Hoosier

The Downtown Heliport is one of the country's first modern helicopter landing fields.

Dome and Market Square Arena are the sites of amateur and professional football and basketball games. The city also has many places used for Olympic training and competition for a variety of sports. These include bike racing, swimming, track and field, rowing, and ice skating. The National Institute for Fitness and Sport, as well as the American College of Sports Medicine, give athletes, coaches, and trainers important information about physical fitness.

Amateur athletics have become very big business in Indianapolis. They have given the city the nickname, "Amateur Sports Capital of the World." Indianapolis has hosted such important amateur events as the 1982 National Sports Festival, the 1987 Pan American Games, and the 1988 Olympic trials in track and field and swimming and diving—to name a very few!

For professional sports fans, the city offers the NFL's Indianapolis Colts and the NBA's Indiana Pacers. It also has the Indianapolis Indians—a Triple-A baseball team—and the Indianapolis Ice—an International Hockey League team.

Because of the number of athletic stadiums and arenas in the city, several amateur sports groups have their headquarters in Indianapolis. The Amateur Athletic Union, the Athletic Congress (for track and field), and several other U.S. Olympic federations all call the city home. These groups represent young American athletes competing

An Indiana high school basketball team takes part in the Boys' State Championships at Market Square Arena.

Downtown workers lunch in City Market Plaza.

on both the national and international level, including the Olympics.

In addition to these organizations, many national insurance companies are based in the city. There are so many insurance companies lining one section of North Meridian Street that it is known as Insurance Row.

One unusual Indianapolis firm is the George F. Cram Company. It is one of the oldest globe and mapmaking companies in the United States. Founded in 1866 by George F. Cram, a Union Army mapmaker during the Civil War, the company has made maps and globes for schools all over North America for more than 100 years.

At the end of World War II, Indianapolis's reputation as the "Toolmaker to the Nation" made the city attractive to many large companies. Ford, Chrysler, RCA, and Western Electric opened factories in the city. Indianapolis's economy slowed in the 1960s, though, and most of the factories had closed by the early 1980s.

Although it is not home to many big companies, modern Indianapolis is known as one of the best places in the country to start a new business. It costs less to rent office and ware-house space than in other cities. It costs less to live in Indianapolis, too. This makes it easier for people to start their own businesses.

This combination of large corporations and small, local companies has helped give Indianapolis one of the lowest unemployment rates in the country. For this and many other reasons, Indianapolis is a good place to live.

# 4

# From Bagels to Baklava

From the time the Mile Square began to take shape, people from around the world have been coming to Indianapolis

The Germans and the Irish had an early effect on Indianapolis. As these two groups settled near each other, neighborhoods grew around them. Many of these people loved music. This led to choirs, orchestras, and community bands. The Indianapolis Symphony Orchestra is still very popular. The strong religious faith of these groups led to many different churches around the city. Several of these remain standing today.

During the 1980s, Indianapolis attracted new residents from Latin America, Asia, and the Middle East. People from North Africa, Japan, and India have come to live, study, and work in the city, too.

An autumn street in the Meridian-Kessler neighborhood.

The International Center was built for these people. The center helps newcomers solve the problems of learning a new language and adjusting to a new country. Each autumn, the center holds the International Festival. The weekend-long celebration features such things as hand-made clothing from Japan, jewelry from Mexico, and art from India. There are many food booths and stage shows, too. Thousands of visitors can eat Greek gyros, Chinese egg rolls, or Turkish baklava while watching Hungarian folk dances or listening to Indian music.

Another fun event is the Indiana Black Expo's Summer Celebration. It attracts not only huge crowds, but national attention. The festival includes sports contests, jazz and pop concerts, and plenty of good food. Thousands of people come to Indiana Black Expo, including famous athletes, actors, and musicians.

In spite of these different ethnic backgrounds, Indianapolis has few ethnic neighborhoods. Instead, most areas are divided according to lifestyles.

Mile Square, for example, is popular with young, single people who work downtown. Old apartment buildings in the area have been cleaned up and many new ones have been built. Once-empty warehouses have now been turned into lofts and studios.

As a result, new businesses have opened in the area. Among these are

This parade is just one of the events at Black Expo's Summer Celebration.

At City Market, vendors sell everything from corned beef to chow mein.

cafes, art galleries, coffee shops, book stores, and clothing stores. In the summer, hot dog vendors roll their shiny silver carts onto street corners all over the Mile Square.

For those who would like more than a hot dog, nearby City Market offers fresh fruits and vegetables, meats, cheeses, coffee beans, and tea leaves. At lunchtime, the market's tables are filled with people eating corned beef, fish stew, salads, or chicken chow mein from its many food stands.

On the eastern edge of the Mile Square is Lockerbie Square, one of the city's best-known neighborhoods. Elegant Victorian homes and modern condominiums share the shady, cobblestone streets.

Lockerbie's most famous resident was poet James Whitcomb Riley. The house at 528 Lockerbie Street in which Riley lived for 23 years is now open to the public. Every year, visitors stop by to see where the man who was known worldwide lived and worked until his death in 1916.

To the northeast of Lockerbie Square is Woodruff Place, another neighborhood made famous by a writer. Booth Tarkington used Woodruff Place as a model for the neigh-

The James Whitcomb Riley House in Lockerbie is open for tours.

borhood he called Amberson Addition in his 1919 Pulitzer Prize-winning novel, *The Magnificent Ambersons.*

Woodruff Place has four wide streets divided by grassy strips of land filled with fountains and statues. The huge old houses here became run-down over several decades. In recent years, though, young couples have bought and fixed many of them.

Other Indianapolis neighborhoods—Irvington, Meridian-Kessler, and Butler-Tarkington—are home to a mixture of young professionals, families, and retired people. The Butler-Tarkington area was named for Ovid Butler, a well-known abolitionist during the Civil War, and for author Booth Tarkington. Both once lived in the neighborhood.

One of the liveliest neighborhoods in northeast Indianapolis is Broad Ripple, located next to the White River. Broad Ripple is the site of Greek, French, Mexican, and Italian restaurants, as well as many popular nightclubs and shops.

Many of Indianapolis's artists, photographers, fashion designers, dancers, and musicians live in Broad Ripple. Its streets are lined with small, well-kept homes, and Broad Ripple Park provides plenty of room to run, swim, play tennis, and picnic.

The far northeast section of Indianapolis is one of the fastest-growing parts of the city. The areas of Keystone Crossing and Castleton are shopping and dining districts. They contain some of the city's most expensive

Fountain Square was named after the fountain placed in the center of a turntable used to reverse the direction of streetcars.

retail centers and houses.

On the south side of Indianapolis are Fountain Square and Fletcher Place. The business district of Fountain Square took its name from the fountain built there in 1889. Fletcher Place was named for Calvin Fletcher, one of the city's early settlers. Today, this area is a neighborhood of mostly working-class homes.

Within the Indianapolis city limits are four communities that were not made a part of Indianapolis when Unigov was formed in 1970. These

are Beech Grove, Lawrence, Southport, and Speedway.

Long known as the site of the annual Indy 500, Speedway is also the home of many factories. Every May, large crowds of racing fans come to watch the drivers test their cars and get ready for the Memorial Day weekend race.

The comfortable neighborhoods and communities that make up Indianapolis are the result of the hard work of residents, government officials, and business leaders. Through neighborhood and community groups, Indianapolis's people have worked to solve housing problems, lower crime rates, and clean up litter and pollution. In Indianapolis, people realize that a city is only as good as its neighborhoods and its residents.

Lockerbie Square is filled with tree-lined, cobblestone streets, and old Victorian homes.

# 5

# The Indianapolis Experience

Indianapolis has long been famous for its friendly people. Lately, it's become known for the fun it offers, too. While there is something for everyone to do in the city, it is an especially good place for the young.

One of the city's most popular attractions is the Children's Museum, located north of Monument Circle. Every year, more than 1.5 million people visit the five-story museum. It calls itself the place "where children grow up...and adults don't have to."

Founded in 1925, the Children's Museum has nine galleries filled with "hands-on" displays. Visitors can explore a cave, sift through an archaeological dig, or travel through space. They can also ride a restored carousel, and watch in wonder as the world's largest water clock whooshes away the time.

A working water clock towers over visitors to the Children's Museum of Indianapolis.

Meanwhile, time stands still at the Benjamin Harrison House a few blocks northeast of the Circle. In 1888, Indianapolis attorney Benjamin Harrison was elected the twenty-third president of the United States. His grandfather, William Henry Harrison, had been elected president, too. Benjamin Harrison served as president for one term, and then returned to practice law in Indianapolis. His former home is now a memorial open to all visitors.

When it comes to memorials, the Madame C.J. Walker Center stands out. To honor her mother's fame in the cosmetics business, Lelia Walker built the block-long office and theater complex on Indiana Avenue in 1927. Recently restored, the Walker Center is now the site of many businesses and cultural events. Jazz concerts, plays, and performing arts classes for young people are held at the center.

A few blocks west of Walker Center is the Indianapolis Zoo. The 60-acre (24-hectare) zoo is a "cageless zoo." This means the animals roam through areas that are meant to look like their natural environments. Elephants, zebras, giraffes, and baboons stalk the African plains. Bottlenose dolphins and beluga whales glide through huge tanks in the Whale and Dolphin Pavilion.

The Indianapolis Zoo, along with the Eiteljorg Museum of American Indian and Western Art, is part of a larger project known as White River State Park. The park, which is still

President Benjamin Harrison campaigned from the front porch of his home, now a memorial open to visitors.

Young Indianapolis residents take a camel ride at the Indianapolis Zoo.

being developed, will be filled with amusement rides, picnic areas, fountains, and playground areas. Drawings and a scale model of what the completed park will look like are on display at the visitors' center on Washington Street.

Also near the White River, on the grounds of the former Eli Lilly family estate, stands the Indianapolis Museum of Art. The museum's park-like surroundings are bright with flowers in the summer, and quiet and filled with the smell of pines in the

winter. Not only is the museum a good place to see collections of historic and modern art from around the world, but the land surrounding it is a lovely place to take a stroll.

The museum's grounds are the site of one of the city's liveliest annual events. Every September, the Penrod Art Fair attracts thousands of visitors to a weekend of outdoor art and craft displays, live music, and dancing.

A month before Penrod, thousands of people from all over the state crowd into the fairgrounds for the Indiana State Fair. The fair features a midway filled with carnival rides and music concerts. It also has a variety of farm-related events. These include a husband-calling contest and a pie-judging competition.

No one event draws bigger crowds than the Indianapolis 500. While it may be hard to get into the track on race day, it is easier during the rest of the year. Visitors to the Speedway can board a bus and tour the 2.5-mile (4-kilometer) oval track. They can also stop by the Motor Speedway Hall of Fame Museum, home of one of the largest collections of race cars in the world.

Indianapolis has many other sites and attractions for sports fans. Two blocks south of the State House on Capitol Avenue, the Hoosier Dome rises like a giant marshmallow. The 60,500-seat dome is the sixth largest stadium in the United States. It is the site of a number of sporting events. College and high school football and

These 80 students and their directors are only one part of the award-winning Indianapolis Children's Choir.

basketball games, indoor track meets, conventions, marching band competitions and rock concerts are all held here.

Across from the Hoosier Dome is the Pan Am Building. It is the site of the Indiana/World Skating Academy, an Olympic-quality ice rink open to everyone from experienced skaters to beginners. Outside the building, skateboarders swoop up and down the plaza. The plaza is often the site of organized skateboard competitions and demonstrations.

While sports have been very important to Indianapolis and its residents, culture has not been forgotten. Theater is very much alive in downtown Indianapolis. On West Washington Street, the Indiana Repertory Theatre houses an acting company by the same name. The company performs everything from Shakespeare to song-and-dance routines on the theater's three stages. On the building's top floor is the Indiana Roof, a beautiful ballroom which is the site of formal dances and some concerts.

Also in downtown Indianapolis is the Circle Theater. When the Indianapolis Symphony Orchestra plays here, the streets around the theater are filled with music lovers.

Among central Indiana musical groups, though, none has gained more attention than the Indianapolis Children's Choir. Formed in 1986, the choir is actually six separate choirs and includes 350 singers between the ages of eight and fourteen. The choir has earned international praise for its performances.

From artworks to workouts, Indianapolis gives its residents and visitors many different kinds of fun. As more people are discovering daily, Indianapolis manages to be both an exciting big city and a quiet small town at the same time. The city people used to call India-No-Place is now someplace well worth finding.

# Places to Visit in Indianapolis

## Museums

The Children's Museum
30th and North Meridian streets
(317) 924-5431
*Hands-on exhibits and displays*

Indianapolis Museum of Art
1200 West 38th Street
(317) 923-1331

Civic and Junior Civic Theaters
(317) 923-4597
*Offers stage productions for children and adults, as well as acting classes*

Herron Gallery
1701 North Pennsylvania Street
(317) 923-3651

Indiana State Museum
202 North Alabama Street
(317) 232-1637

Indianapolis Motor Speedway Hall of Fame Museum
4790 West 16th Street
(317) 241-2500

## Historical Attractions

Connor Prairie
13400 Allisonville Road
Noblesville, Indiana
(317) 776-6000
*Historic settlement*

President Benjamin Harrison Memorial Home
1230 North Delaware Street
(317) 631-1898

James Whitcomb Riley House
528 Lockerbie Street
(317) 631-5885

Indiana War Memorial
431 North Meridian Street
(317) 635-1964
*A five-block-long complex commemorating Indiana's soldiers; the Memorial Shrine Building details the history of the region's involvement in wars from the Battle of Tippecanoe to the present*

## Special Places

The Indianapolis Zoo
1200 West Washington Street
(317) 630-2030

City-County Building
200 East Washington Street
(317) 236-3200
*An observatory on the 28th floor*

Indiana State Fairgrounds
1202 East 38th Street
(317) 232-3140

Indiana State House
West Market Street at Capitol Avenue
(317) 927-7500

## Sports

Hoosier Dome/Indianapolis Convention
Center
100 South Capitol Avenue
(317) 262-3452

Market Square Arena
300 East Market Street
(317) 639-6411

Indiana University Natatorium and Track
& Field Stadium
901 West New York Street
(317) 274-3517

Bush Stadium
1501 West 16th Street
(317) 632-5371
*Home of the Indianapolis Indians*

Major Taylor Velodrome
3649 Cold Springs Road
(317) 926-8356
*Named for the first African-American cycling champion, Indianapolis native Marshall "Major" Taylor*

Eagle Creek Park & Reservoir
7840 West 56th Street
(317) 293-4827
*Rowing, hiking, swimming, golfing, archery, sailing, canoeing, and fishing*

## Performing Arts

Circle Theater
45 Monument Circle
(317) 635-6541
*Indianapolis Symphony Orchestra, other musical events*

Indiana Repertory Theatre
140 West Washington Street
(317) 635-5277

Additional information can be obtained from these agencies:

Indianapolis City Center
201 South Capitol Avenue
Indianapolis, IN  46204
(317) 237-5200

Indianapolis Chamber of Commerce
320 North Meridian Street
Indianapolis, IN  46204
(317) 267-2900

# Indianapolis: A Historical Time Line

1820   State commissioners choose the site of Indiana's new state capital

1821   Alexander Ralston designs the Mile Square and the Circle

1825   The first stagecoach arrives in Indianapolis

1832   Indianapolis incorporates as a town; the National Road reaches Indianapolis

1847   Indianapolis residents elect their first mayor

1855   North Western Christian University (now Butler University) is founded

1876   Eli Lilly begins a small prescription drug company

1878   The belt line railroad gives trains access to factories throughout Indianapolis

1888   Indianapolis attorney Benjamin Harrison is elected president of the United States

1899   Carriage maker Charles Black makes the city's first automobile

1902   The Soldiers and Sailors Monument is dedicated

1911   The first Indianapolis 500 auto race is won by Ray Harroun

1919   Booth Tarkington publishes his Pulitzer Prize-winning novel, *The Magnificent Ambersons*

1925   The Children's Museum is founded

1927   The Madame C.J. Walker Center is built

1929   Indianapolis jazz fan Hoagy Carmichael writes "Stardust"

| | |
|---|---|
| 1950 | The Western Electric Company begins manufacturing telephones in Indianapolis |
| 1970 | Indiana and Marion County become one community under Unigov |
| 1982 | The National Sports Festival is held in Indianapolis for the first time |
| 1983 | The Hoosier Dome opens |
| 1984 | Professional football's Baltimore Colts move west and become the Indianapolis Colts |
| 1985 | The Indianapolis Downtown Heliport opens |
| 1986 | The renovated Union Station opens |
| 1987 | The Pan American Games are held in Indianapolis |
| 1988 | The Indianapolis Zoo opens its new, 60-acre cageless zoo |
| 1989 | The Children's Museum expands, opening new galleries; The Eiteljorg Museum of American Indian and Western Art opens |

# Index